WISE OLD OWL'S HALLOWEEN ADVENTURE

by ROBERT KRAUS

PICTURES BY ROBERT AND PAMELA KRAUS

Troll Associates

FOR PARKER

It was Halloween in the Magic Forest. All the forest creatures were out trick or treating. All but one.

3

Wise Old Owl was bent over his typewriter, working on a story. It was a mystery set in the deep, dark woods late one Halloween night. The beloved author had nearly finished his tale when he heard a rapping at his door.

Rap! Rap! Rap!

Wise Old Owl scurried downstairs and flung open the front door. Before his eyes stood Wendy Witch.

"Trick or treat?" asked Wise Old Owl.

"No, your pizza delivery!" she said.

"Why I'd almost forgotten!" hooted Wise Old Owl who never, *ever* forgot a birdseed pizza.

He sat down for a quick bite—
Mmmm! Mmmm! Good!—
and raced back upstairs to finish his bone-
chilling story.

When he got to the top of the stairs, Wise Old
Owl's eyes opened wide. "My typewriter is
gone!" he gasped. "How will I ever finish my
story?"

Quickly, he dialed 911.

"Police Chief Pelican," answered a deep voice.
"You lose it—we find it!"

"Wise Old Owl, here," said Wise Old Owl. "I'm
calling to report a lost typewriter."

"Haven't seen a typewriter, lately. In fact, I
haven't seen one in years," said the chief. "I'm
surprised you don't use a laptop, Wise Old Owl."

"I guess I'm just an old-fashioned owl," sighed
Wise Old Owl.

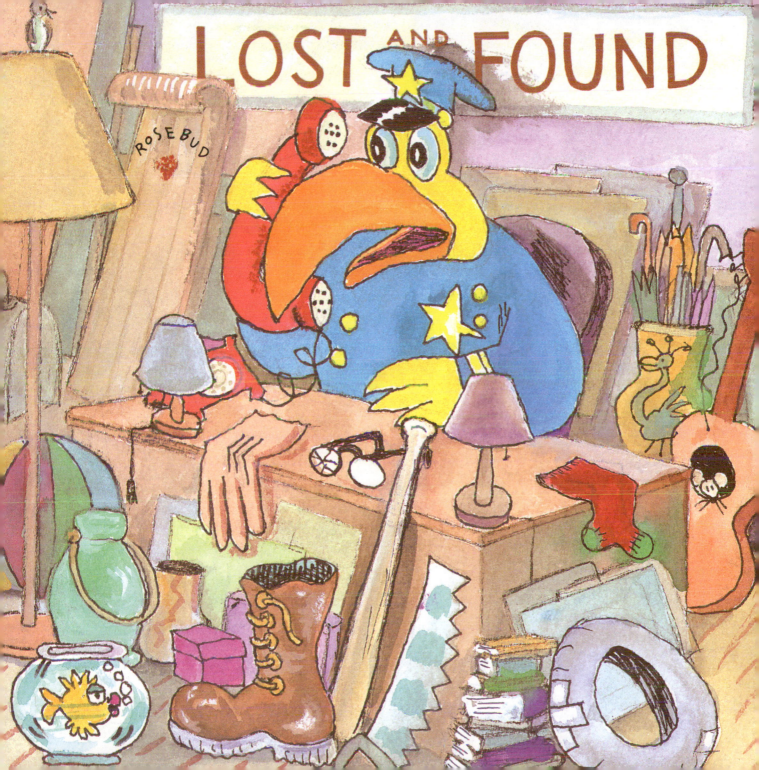

Quickly, Wise Old Owl grabbed his hat and his scarf and raced into the forest. He hadn't gone far when he saw a group of trick-or-treaters— his loyal fans.

"Trick or treat!" they sang out.

Luckily, Wise Old Owl had a supply of Tweet Tweet candy bars on hand. First he gave a treat to each trickster. Then he asked for clues to help him in his search.

"They went that-a way!"

"Which-a way?"

"This-a way!"

"That-a way!"

Wise Old Owl was very confused. He thanked his young friends and continued to run deep into the woods.

Suddenly, out of a tree dropped Slow Turtle.
"Care for a little bungee jumping?" he asked.
"Later, Turtle," groaned Wise Old Owl. "Right
now, I'm very upset. My typewriter has disappeared."
"I can help you find it," Slow Turtle said.

14

Using the skills he had learned in the woods,
Slow Turtle put his ear to the ground.

"The better to hear," he said. Then they both
heard a *tap, tap, tapping*.

"Someone is tapping on my typewriter," said
Wise Old Owl. "I would know that sound
anywhere!"

17

The two detectives followed the sound—
TAP!   TAP!   TAP!—
till at last they came to an old oak tree.

"Come out, you culprit!" hooted Wise Old Owl.
"I hear you tapping on my typewriter."

19

"Tapping on your typewriter? I'm tapping on a tree," echoed a voice above them. "My dinner's in here somewhere." It was Woodruff Woodpecker. "My apologies," said Wise Old Owl.

20

Sad and weary, Wise Old Owl sat down
beneath the tree. He wondered if he would ever
see his typewriter again.

The full moon was shining brightly when Slow
Turtle spotted something strange. "Wise Old

Owl," he said, "how can you be sitting here and
be flying through the sky at the same time?"

"I can't, Slow Turtle," said Wise Old Owl.

"Then who is that?" asked Slow Turtle.

Above them was a flying creature dressed up
as Wise Old Owl. And it was carrying a
typewriter!

Wise Old Owl hopped on Wendy Witch's broomstick and chased his look-alike across the Halloween sky.

"Pull over," he hooted.

The flying creature landed upside down on a
tree limb. Then Wise Old Owl got an ever bigger
surprise. The creature was Matt the bat.

"What are you doing with my typewriter?" hooted
Wise Old Owl. "And why are you dressed like me?"

"Oh, beloved author," said Matt the bat. "I was tired of being a bat on Halloween. Anyone can be a bat. But hardly anyone gets to be a beloved author."

"But you took my typewriter!" said Wise Old Owl.

"I can't be an author without a typewriter," Matt replied.

"The only thing an author needs is a good idea," said Wise Old Owl.

"You're so wise," said Wendy Witch.

"You're both right!" Matt squeaked. "I'll fly your typewriter home right now by Bat Express. I'm sorry I took it."

Wise Old Owl accepted Matt's apology. Then he waved good-bye to Slow Turtle. "Happy Halloween," he hooted.

"Let's go camping, sometime," croaked Slow Turtle.

"What a Halloween adventure!"
said the beloved author as he hopped
onto Wendy Witch's broomstick. "You
never know what is going to happen
next."

Wise Old Owl read the story he had been writing. "Too boring!" he hooted.

So he sat down at his typewriter and wrote a new story. It was full of suspense and surprises, twists and turns, fun and excitement—just like real life!